Luke and the Mule

Written by
Jill Atkins

Illustrated by
Andy Hamilton

Luke's home was outside the town.

He had no car and no bike.

Each time he went into town, his feet hurt.

He wished he had something to ride.

One day, Luke saw a white card.

It said,

> Help! Duchess June is sad.
> There's a prize if you can amuse her.
> Duke Harold.

Luke went to the home of Duke Harold and Duchess June.

It was a fantastic dwelling!

Luke tapped on the gate.

A man dressed in black turned up. He was the butler.

"Is this Duchess June's home?" asked Luke.

"Yes," said the butler.

"Is she sad?" Luke asked.

"She is," said the butler. "Now come in and meet the duke."

"What's the prize if I amuse the duchess?" Luke asked.

"A mule," said the duke. "It's cute!"

Luke grinned. A cute mule was just what he needed!

"What must I do to amuse her?" he asked.

"You must sing a tune," said the duke.

"Oh dear!" said Luke. "I can't sing at all! I sound like a toad."

"Good day to you, then," said the duke. The butler led Luke out.

When Luke got home, he tried to sing a tune.

Croak, Croak, Croak!

"That's no good!" he said. So he asked a rat to sing with him.

Croak, Squeak, Croak!

"That's no better," he cried. "But I do need that mule!"

He asked a goat to join in.

Croak, Squeak, Bleat!

Luke shook his head. Then he grinned.

"We've tried hard," he said to the rat and the goat. "Now let's see how we get on."

They all ran to the home of the duke and duchess.

"I think we can amuse Duchess June," Luke said to the butler.

The butler took them to meet the duchess. She did look sad!

"Can we sing a tune for you?" he asked.

"Yes," she said.

They stood near her chair and sang.

Croak, Squeak, Bleat!

Duchess June clapped her hands on her ears.

"That's **so bad!**" she exclaimed. Then she grinned and jumped for joy.

"It's **so bad**, it makes me feel much, much better!" she said.

Then the duke came in.

"Thank you," said the duke. "You have amused the duchess, so you shall have the prize."

Luke felt good as he set off home on his cute mule.

The next day, Luke, the rat, the goat and the cute mule formed a band.

Croak, Squeak, Bleat, Groan!

They were a big hit in the town. Even Duchess June came to see them play!